For Grant, Mark and Tammy
J.F.

For Jem, Anne, Benjamin and Rose
P.M.

First published in 1992 by J.M. Dent & Sons Ltd.
Published as a Dolphin Paperback in 1999
by Orion Children's Books
a division of the Orion Publishing Group Ltd
Orion House
5 Upper St Martin's Lane
London WC2H 9EA
Text copyright © Jenni Fleetwood, 1992
Illustrations copyright © Peter Melnyczuk, 1992

The right of Jenni Fleetwood and Peter Melnyczuk
to be identified as the Author and the Illustrator of this work
has been asserted by them in accordance
with the Copyright, Designs and Patents Act 1988.

Printed in Italy

British Library Cataloguing in Publication Data is available.

The illustrations for this book were prepared using coloured inks, pencils and pastels.

~*While Shepherds Watched*~

Jenni Fleetwood · Illustrated by Peter Melnyczuk

Dolphin

It got dark suddenly. One minute
Matthias could see the rocks and grass
on the hilllside, the next even the sheep
were just shadows.

Matthias shivered with excitement.
It was the first time he had been
allowed to spend all night in the fields
with the other shepherd boys.

He pulled his sheepskin jacket close
around his body and felt for his new
whistle. His father had carved it for
him and Matthias was very proud of it.

The sheep were huddling together for warmth. One sheep stood apart from the rest.

'What's the matter with that one?' asked Matthias.

'Never seen a lamb born, Matt?' said John.

He was one of the older boys.

'No'.

'It's fantastic,' said John, turning to the pool of light in the darkness where the older lads had made a fire. They were playing a game with pebbles, throwing them into the air. Matthias did not join them. It was comfortable here, next to the sheep.

The lamb wasn't born until after midnight. By then the ewe was exhausted. She licked her baby gently but the lamb made no sound and did not try to get to its feet.

Matthias wished there was more light. He wanted to see the lamb; to find out if there was anything he could do to help it.

And then there was light, blinding rays of it. Below them, Bethlehem looked as it always did – a hamlet of honey-gold houses. The light had not come from there. It seemed to be pouring from the sky itself.

Suddenly a figure appeared in the field. It seemed part of the light, white and clear and brilliant.

The shepherds were very frightened. All except Matthias, who was too worried about the mother sheep and lamb to think about anything else.

The figure in white said 'Don't be afraid, I have good news for you. Today, in the city of David, a Saviour has been born. You will find the baby lying in a manger.'

The sound of singing was all around them as the figure faded. But the light did not go. The field was still bright, and when he looked up Matthias saw a star shining over Bethlehem, the place that people called the city of David.

There was silence. Then everybody
spoke at once.

'What was that?'

'Was it a vision. Was that an angel?'

'Do you think it's true about the
baby?'

And then John's voice, louder than
the rest: 'Let's go and see. Come on
Matthias! There's nothing you can do
for that lamb!'

'It's all right. I'll stay.'

Matthias did not want to leave.
The ewe had made no attempt to feed
her baby. The lamb was shivering and
had laid its head on his knee.

Matthias suddenly changed his mind. He opened his jerkin and tucked the little creature against his chest to keep it safe.

The starlight made it easy to follow the path. When he caught up with the others they were already entering the town.

John had stopped to talk to two young girls.

'They say there's a baby born. Maybe the promised Saviour.'

'Where?'

'In the stable, behind the inn.'

'The stable?'

'The inn was full. Come on!'

They joined a stream of townsfolk
pressing down the dusty track.

It was just an ordinary stable, but
the starlight was so bright that
Matthias could see every detail. Ever
afterwards he could picture it clearly
in his memory.

Matthias hung back, but the people
behind were pushing hard and he was
soon jostled through the doorway.

Inside, he could see a donkey and a cow and a few goats. Hay stood in bales, its sweet scent filling the air. In a corner, bathed in the yellow glow of a candle, sat a family. A father and a mother, holding a tiny baby.

Matthias wanted to see the child properly, but there were too many people in front of him. He jumped up, forgetting for a moment the lamb against his chest, so still was that small body against his.

The baby's mother saw him and asked others to move so that he could come closer.

The child was wrapped in cloth.
Matthias was disappointed. He didn't
know what he had expected, but
certainly more than this.

He leant forward and as he did so
his jacket fell open and a small damp
head peeped out. The baby reached
out and touched the lamb.

'He's only just been born,'
Matthias told the woman.

'Like my son,' she replied softly.
She smiled and Matthias felt
something fizz inside him. He
laughed and the baby laughed too.

Matthias wanted to give the child something, but what? And then he remembered his whistle. He put it in the manger.

'Thank you,' said the baby's mother.

Matthias was full of joy. He jumped up and ran out of the stable and up the path to the fields, the lamb bumping softly against him.

*There was a dark shape by the gate.
It was the mother sheep. Matthias
opened his jacket and set the lamb
down on the ground. It looked around
for a moment, took a couple of shaky
steps, then moved quickly to its
mother, its tail wagging as it tasted
milk for the first time.*

*The boy looked at the ewe and her
healthy little lamb and then turned
back to see the town of Bethlehem. In
the silver light of the star it lay still
and silent.*

It had been a night for miracles.